THE  MOTHER GOOSE

WINDMILL
BOOKS
INCORPORATED

Published by Windmill Books, Inc.
Distributed by Harper & Row

J
811
M-A

THE CHAS. ADDAMS MOTHER GOOSE
Copyright © 1967 by Charles Addams

Printed in the United States of America. All rights reserved. No part of this
book may be used or reproduced in any manner whatsoever without written
permission except in the case of brief quotations embodied
in critical articles and reviews.

LIBRARY OF CONGRESS CATALOG CARD NUMBER: 67-24372

58979

Humpty Dumpty sat on a wall;

Humpty Dumpty had a great fall.

All the king's horses and all the king's men
Cannot put Humpty Dumpty together again.

Three blind mice, see how they run!

    They all ran after the farmer's wife,

Who cut off their tails with a carving knife.

    Did you ever see such a sight in your life

As three blind mice?

Little Miss Muffet
  Sat on a tuffet,
Eating her curds and whey.
  There came a big spider,
Who sat down beside her
  And frightened Miss Muffet away.

Tom, Tom, the piper's son,
    Stole a pig and away did run;
The pig was eat, and Tom was beat,
    Till he run crying down the street.

One misty, moisty morning,
    When cloudy was the weather,
There I met an old man
    Clothed all in leather—
Clothed all in leather
    With cap under his chin.
How do you do, and how do you do,
    And how do you do again?

There was an old woman
Lived under a hill,
And if she isn't gone,
She lives there still.

Pease porridge hot,
    Pease porridge cold,
Pease porridge in the pot nine days old.
    Some like it hot,
Some like it cold,
    Some like it in the pot nine days old.

Sing a song of sixpence, a pocket full of rye;
    Four and twenty blackbirds baked in a pie.
When the pie was opened, the birds began to sing:
    Wasn't that a dainty dish to set before the king?
The king was in the countinghouse, counting out his money;
    The queen was in the parlor, eating bread and honey;
The maid was in the garden, hanging out the clothes,
    When down came a blackbird and snapped off her nose.

Dickory, dickory, dare!
The pig flew up in the air;
The man in brown soon brought him down.
Dickory, dickory, dare!

Hickory, dickory, dock!
The mouse ran up the clock;

The clock struck one,
And down he run.
Hickory, dickory, dock!

I do not like thee, Doctor Fell;

The reason why I cannot tell.

But this I know, and know full well;

I do not like thee, Doctor Fell.

Solomon Grundy, Born on Monday,   Christened on Tuesday,

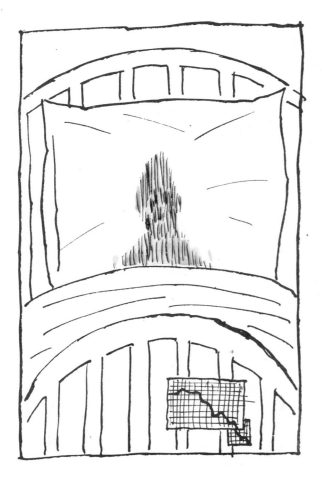

Worse on Friday,   Died on Saturday,

Married on Wednesday,

Took ill on Thursday,

Buried on Sunday.

This is the end
Of Solomon Grundy.

This is the house that Jack built.

B

This is the malt
That lay in the house that Jack built.

C

This is the rat
That ate the malt
That lay in the house that Jack built.

D

This is the cat
That killed the rat
That ate the malt
That lay in the house that Jack built.

E

This is the dog
That worried the cat
That killed the rat
That ate the malt
That lay in the house that Jack built.

F

This is the cow with the crumpled horn,
That tossed the dog
That worried the cat
That killed the rat
That ate the malt
That lay in the house that Jack built.

G

This is the maiden all forlorn,
That milked the cow with the crumpled horn,
That tossed the dog
That worried the cat
That killed the rat
That ate the malt
That lay in the house that Jack built.

H

This is the man all tattered and torn,
    That kissed the maiden all forlorn,
That milked the cow with the crumpled horn,
    That tossed the dog
That worried the cat
    That killed the rat
That ate the malt
    That lay in the house that Jack built.

I

This is the priest all shaven and shorn,
    That married the man all tattered and torn,
That kissed the maiden all forlorn,
    That milked the cow with the crumpled horn,
That tossed the dog
    That worried the cat
That killed the rat
    That ate the malt
That lay in the house that Jack built.

J

This is the cock that crowed in the morn,
    That waked the priest all shaven and shorn,
That married the man all tattered and torn,
    That kissed the maiden all forlorn,
That milked the cow with the crumpled horn,
    That tossed the dog
That worried the cat
    That killed the rat
That ate the malt
    That lay in the house that Jack built.

K

This is the farmer sowing his corn,
    That kept the cock that crowed in the morn,
That waked the priest all shaven and shorn,
    That married the man all tattered and torn,
That kissed the maiden all forlorn,
    That milked the cow with the crumpled horn,
That tossed the dog
    That worried the cat
That killed the rat
    That ate the malt
That lay in the house that Jack built.

Little King Pippin he built a fine hall,
   Pie-crust and pastry-crust that was the wall.
The windows were made of black pudding and white
   And slated with pancakes, you ne'er saw the like.

Girls and boys,
　　Come out to play.
The moon does shine
　　As bright as day.
Come with a hoop,
　　Come with a call,
Come with a good will,
　　Or not at all.

Mistress Mary, quite contrary,
    How does your garden grow?
With silver bells and cockleshells
    And pretty maids all in a row.

Rain, rain, go away,
  Come again another day.

St. Dunstan, as the story goes,
   Once pulled the devil by the nose
With red hot tongs, which made him roar,
   That could be heard ten miles or more.

Fishy, fishy in the brook,
    Daddy catch him on a hook,
Mommy fry him in a pan,
    Johnny eat him like a man.

There was an old woman tossed in a basket,
    Seventeen times as high as the moon;
But where she was going no mortal could tell,
    For under her arm she carried a broom.
"Old woman, old woman, old woman," said I,
    "Whither, oh whither, oh whither so high?"
"To sweep the cobwebs from the sky,
    And I'll be with you by-and-by."

Jack Sprat
    Could eat no fat;
His wife could eat no lean.
    And so, betwixt them both,
They licked the platter clean.

Bat, bat,
 Come under my hat,
And I'll give you a slice of bacon;
 And when I bake,
I'll give you a cake
 If I am not mistaken.

Pretty John Watts,
    We are troubled with rats;
Will you drive them out of the house?
    We have mice too in plenty
That feast in the pantry,
    But let them stay
And nibble away.
    What harm is a little brown mouse?

As I was going to St. Ives,
    I met a man with seven wives.
Each wife had seven sacks,
    Each sack had seven cats,
Each cat had seven kits.
    Kits, cats, sacks, and wives,
How many were going to St. Ives?

Here am I,
　　Little Jumping Joan;
When nobody's with me,
　　I'm all alone.

Wee Willie Winkie
    Runs through the town,
Upstairs and downstairs
    In his nightgown,
Rapping at the window,
    Crying through the lock,
"Are the children all in bed,
    For now it's eight o'clock?"

Old Mother Goose, when
　　She wanted to wander,
Would ride through the air
　　On a very fine gander.

Date Due

MR 28'68	MAR 5 '78	FEB 7 '81	OCT 15 '84	OCT 3 1 1988
NO 18'69	MAR 18 '78	OCT 29 '81	FEB 27 '85	FEB 2 3 1989
OC 8'70	APR 28 '78	MAR 03 '82	OCT 20 '85	OCT 2 6 1989
OC 20'70	MAR 18 '79	OCT 06 1982	FEB 17 '86	DEC 0 6 1990
FE 14'74	APR 09 '79	OCT 14 1982	OCT 8 '86	MAR 2 3 1991
OC 23'75	OCT 1 '79	FEB 12 1983	OCT 23 '86	
MAR 10'77	OCT 22 '79	MAR 12 1983	OCT 27 '86	MAR 3 0 1992
JUL 20'77	MAR 23 '80	FEB 21 '84	NOV 04 1987	
NOV 20'77	NOV 14 '80	FEB 27 '84	DEC 23 1987	
			DEC 0 2 1991	

PRINTED IN U.S.A. CAT. NO. 23 231

J
811
M-A

58979

Mother Goose
The Chas. Addams Mother Goose

LIBRARY
OHIO DOMINICAN COLLEGE
COLUMBUS, OHIO 43219